Halloween

BY ANN HEINRICHS • ILLUSTRATED BY TERI WEIDNER

Published by The Child's World®
1980 Lookout Drive • Mankato, MN 56003-1705
800-599-READ • www.childsworld.com

Acknowledgments
The Child's World®: Mary Berendes, Publishing Director
The Design Lab: Design
Jody Jensen Shaffer: Editing

ISBN 9781623235079
LCCN 2013931402

Printed in the United States of America
Mankato, MN
July, 2013
PA02169

ABOUT THE AUTHOR

Ann Heinrichs lives in Chicago, Illinois.
She has written more than two hundred
books for children. She loves traveling to
faraway places.

ABOUT THE ILLUSTRATOR

Teri Weidner illustrated this spooky book
using pastels and colored pencils. She
lives with her husband Chris and their son
Nicholas in Portsmouth, New Hampshire.

Table of Contents

Costumes, pumpkins, and candy
are all part of the excitement
of Halloween.

CHAPTER 1
Trick or Treat!

Witches and ghosts dangle in windows. Black cats lurk in the bushes. Jack-o'-lanterns glow with a toothy grin. Boo! It's Halloween!

Kids in costumes run giggling down the street. They ring their neighbors' doorbells. What a sight they are as they shout "Trick or Treat!"

CHAPTER 2

A Scary Night

How did we get Halloween? It's a long story! It began with the **ancient** Celtic people. They once lived in Great Britain and Ireland.

November 1 was the Celtic New Year. The night before, Celts held a festival. It was called *Samhain* (SOW-en).

Celts believed the spirits of the dead rose up that night. They roamed around causing trouble. How could people scare them off? By wearing costumes!

People tried to look as scary as could be. Some even wore animal heads. They made lots of noise, too. They had to scare those spirits away!

For the New Year, the Celts lit bonfires, or huge, open-air fires. The bonfires blazed on hilltops. They believed this would help scare the bad spirits away. The Celts also left food on their doorsteps for good spirits.

For Celts, Samhain was a time to scare spirits away.

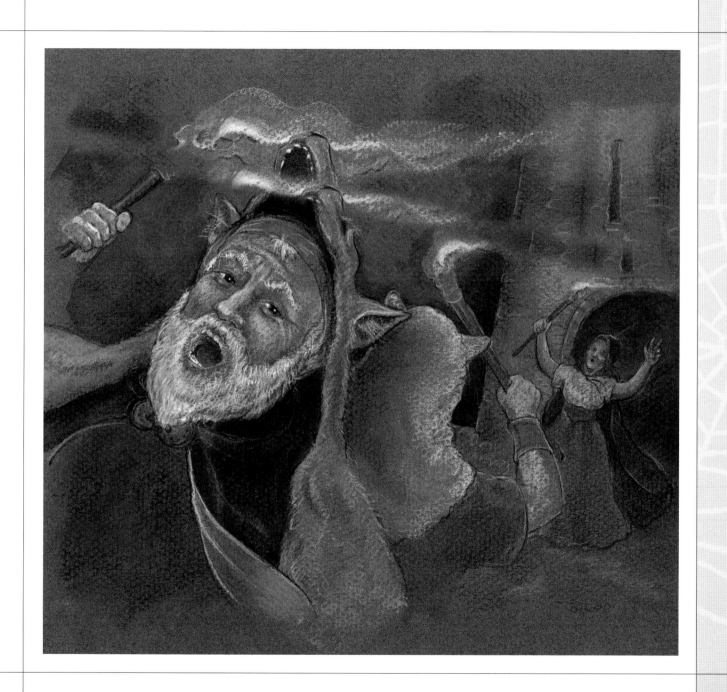

CHAPTER 3

Roman Festivals

Many other ancient people held fall festivals. Fall was the time to gather crops. People celebrated their **harvests** then.

Some ancient harvest festivals took place during the harvest moon. That's the full moon that rises in September. This marks the first day of autumn.

Ancient fall festivals were a celebration of harvesttime.

Ancient Romans held Feralia in October. This was a time to honor the dead. Another Roman festival honored Pomona. She was the **goddess** of fruit and trees. Her **symbol** was the apple.

The Romans took over Celtic lands. They joined their fall festivals with Samhain. Then everyone's customs got jumbled together!

Ancient Romans had another fall harvest festival called *Cerelia* (suh-RAY-lee-uh). Cerelia honored Ceres (SIHR-eez). She was the goddess of crops, especially grains. Our word cereal comes from "Ceres."

CHAPTER 4
All Hallows' Eve

In time, Christian beliefs spread through Europe. Old beliefs died out. But people still liked their **traditional** fall festivals.

Christian leaders used this. They simply changed the festivals' meanings. They made November 1 All Saints' Day. It was also called All Hallows' Day. Something hallowed is considered holy. All Hallows' Day was meant to honor the Christian saints.

The night before was October 31. That was All Hallows' Eve. Some people called it All Hallows' Evening or E'en. And that became the word *Halloween*!

The Christian Church declared November 1 All Saints' Day in about the year 837.

Christian beliefs eventually replaced the meaning behind ancient fall festivals.

CHAPTER 5

Costumes, Mischief, Apples, and Fun

Irish and British people eventually became Christians. Still, they kept some old customs. October 31 might be All Hallows' Eve. But it was still a scary night. That's when spirits roamed around.

People dressed as witches and ghosts. And they caused lots of **mischief**. It all helped scare the spirits away.

Apples were also part of Halloween. They recalled the Roman goddess Pomona. Bobbing for apples became a Halloween game. People floated

In some parts of Ireland, Halloween is called Pooky Night. It's named after a fairy called the *pookah*. Pookahs were said to be full of mischief!

Bobbing for apples is a tasty and challenging Halloween tradition!

Candy-coated apples are another Halloween treat.

apples in a tub of water. Then they tried to grab the apples with their teeth. Candy-coated apples became Halloween treats, too.

Immigrants brought their Halloween customs to the United States. These customs lost their old meanings over time. They simply became ways to

Witches, bats, and black cats all help to make Halloween spooky!

have fun. Halloween continued to be a night for scary things. Like what? Witches, skeletons, black cats, spiders, and bats!

Black Cats

In some places, black cats are a sign of good luck. Fishermen's wives in Yorkshire, England, used to keep a black cat at home when their husbands went to sea. This would assure their safe return.

CHAPTER 6

Begging for Treats

November 2 became a Christian holiday, too. It was named All Souls' Day. That was a day to honor the dead.

Christians in Europe went "souling" that day. They traveled from village to village, knocking on doors. At each house, they begged a different family for soul cakes. Those were little squares of bread with berries inside. The beggars made promises in return. They would pray for the family's dead loved ones.

This custom eventually came to the United States. It became part of Halloween. Now, children go trick-or-treating. They beg for candy treats!

People in Europe used to get soul cakes on November 2.

CHAPTER 7

The Jack-o'-Lantern

There's an Irish folk tale about a man named Jack. He played tricks on the devil. After Jack died, the devil got even. He made Jack wander around at night. Jack could use only a tiny light to see where he was going. This light was a burning lump of coal. Jack carried it inside a hollowed-out turnip.

This folk tale led to an Irish Halloween custom. People carved out a turnip, potato, or beet. Inside, they put a glowing lump of coal. They called it Jack's Lantern, or Jack of the Lantern. That became the word *jack-o'-lantern*!

Pumpkins are native to North and Central America. Irish immigrants discovered pumpkins in the United States. They found that pumpkins were easy to carve into jack-o'-lanterns.

Carving jack-o'-lanterns is a popular Halloween activity.

Many Irish people moved to the United States. Once there, they used big pumpkins for the lanterns.

Today, many people make jack-o'-lanterns on Halloween. They just carve a scary face on a pumpkin and put a candle inside.

Día de los Muertos is a happy time. Family and friends joyfully recall a loved one's life.

CHAPTER 8

The Day of the Dead

Mexicans celebrate *Día de los Muertos* (DEE-ah day lohs MWEHR-tohs). That means "day of the dead." It falls on November 2—All Souls' Day. Both All Souls' Day and Día de los Muertos are meant to honor loved ones who have died. But Día de los Muertos celebrations begin days before November 2.

This festival fits right in with Halloween. Children wear skeleton costumes. And people eat candy shaped like skulls. They also make **altars** to the dead. They're decorated with candles, flowers, and photos. It's not a sad festival at all. It celebrates a loved one's life!

CHAPTER 9

Poetry Corner

The Witches Song

Hoity-toity!
Hop-o'-my-thumb!
Tweedledee and Tweedledum!
All hobgoblins come to me,
Over the mountains,
    over the sea:
Come in a hurry,
    come in a crowd,
Flying, chattering,
    shrieking loud...
Thus said a witch
    on a windy night,
Then sailed on her broomstick
    out of sight.

—Ruth Bedford (1882–1963)

FIVE LITTLE PUMPKINS

Five little pumpkins sitting on a gate.

The first one said, "Oh my, it's getting late."

The second one said, "There are witches in the air."

The third one said, "But we don't care!"

The fourth one said, "Let's run and run and run."

The fifth one said, "I'm ready for some fun!"

Woooo, went the wind

And out went the light

And the five little pumpkins rolled out of sight!

—*Author unknown*

THREE LITTLE WITCHES

One little, two little, three little witches,
Flying over haystacks, flying over ditches,
Slid down the moon without any hitches.
Hi-ho, Halloween's here!

One little, two little, three little witches,
Flew by a fence and tore their britches;
Had to go home and get some stitches.
Hi-ho, Halloween's here.

—*Author unknown*

TRICK OR TREAT!

Out we go
To Trick or Treat—
We don't care who
    we will meet.

Witches, goblins,
Ghosts in a sheet—
We're scary too,
    from head to feet.

Owls are hooting,
Bat wings beat—
But nothing can stop us
    from Trick or Treat!

Give us an apple.
That would be neat.
Or give us something
    really sweet.

We will share
What we get to eat,
Just so we get to go
    Trick or Treat!

—*Author unknown*

Joining in the Spirit of Halloween

* Is there a pumpkin farm in your area? Visit the farm and pick out a pumpkin. Then chat with the farmers. Ask how many Halloween pumpkins they sell.

* Draw a face on your pumpkin with a magic marker. Then have a grown-up help you carve around the lines you have drawn.

* Is there a children's hospital in your community? Visit the children before Halloween. Bring craft materials and help them make decorations.

* Do you know a Mexican American? Ask how he or she celebrates Día de los Muertos.

Making Spooky Spiders

What you need:

1 cup semi-sweet chocolate chips
   or butterscotch chips
2 cups chow-mein noodles
$^1/_2$ cup pecans, peanuts, or walnut pieces

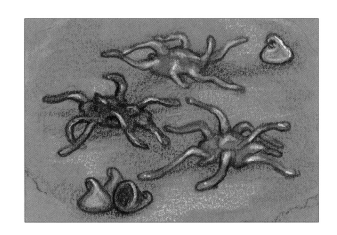

Directions

1. Place the chocolate or butterscotch chips in a small saucepan.
   Melt over low heat on the stove top.*
2. Stir until the liquid chocolate or butterscotch is smooth.
   Remove the pan from the stove top.
3. Mix in the chow-mein noodles and nuts so that they're coated
   in chocolate or butterscotch.
4. Lay a piece of wax paper on a baking sheet. Using a teaspoon,
   place about 24 small pieces of the mixture onto the baking sheet.
5. Chill in the refrigerator for about 15 minutes and then remove.
   Eek—your spiders have legs! Don't worry. It's just the noodles.
6. Store your tasty treats in a cool place.

Have an adult help you operate the stove.

Making Egg-Carton Spiders

These easy-to-make spiders are sure to add a scary touch to your Halloween celebration.

What you need:

1 paint brush

Black paint

Scissors

An egg carton

Hole punch

Black pipe cleaners

Wire cutters

Wiggle eyes

Glue

Directions

1. Have an adult help you cut the egg carton apart so that you have several little cups or sections.
2. Have an adult help you cut the pipe cleaners in half.
3. Use the hole punch to make eight holes in the bottom edge of an egg-carton section.
4. Paint the egg-carton cup with black paint and let it dry.
5. Put a piece of pipe cleaner through a hole in one side of the egg-carton section and out through the opposite hole. Bend the sides of the stem down. Do this three more times until you have all eight legs in place.
6. Glue on the wiggle eyes.

Now you're ready to scare up some fun. Happy Halloween!

Glossary

altars—tables set up to honor someone

ancient—from the very distant past

goddess—a female honored as a god

harvests—crops that have been gathered

immigrants—people who move to another country

mischief—trouble or tricks

symbol—an object that stands for an idea

traditional—following long-held customs

Learn More

Books

Axelrod-Contrada, Jean. *Halloween and Day of the Dead Traditions around the World*. Mankato, MN: The Child's World, 2013.

Ghigna, Charles, and Adam McCauley (illustrator). *Twenty-One Spooktacular Poems*. Philadelphia, PA: Running Press Kids, 2003.

Mills, Claudia, and Catherine Stock. *Gus and Grandpa and the Halloween Costume*. New York: Farrar, Straus and Giroux, 2002.

Park, Barbara, and Denise Brunkus (illustrator). *Junie B., First Grader: Boo...and I Mean It!* New York: Random House, 2004.

Web Sites

Visit our Web site for links about Halloween and other holidays:

childsworld.com/links

Note to Parents, Teachers, and Librarians: We routinely verify our Web links to make sure they are safe and active sites. So encourage your readers to check them out!

Index